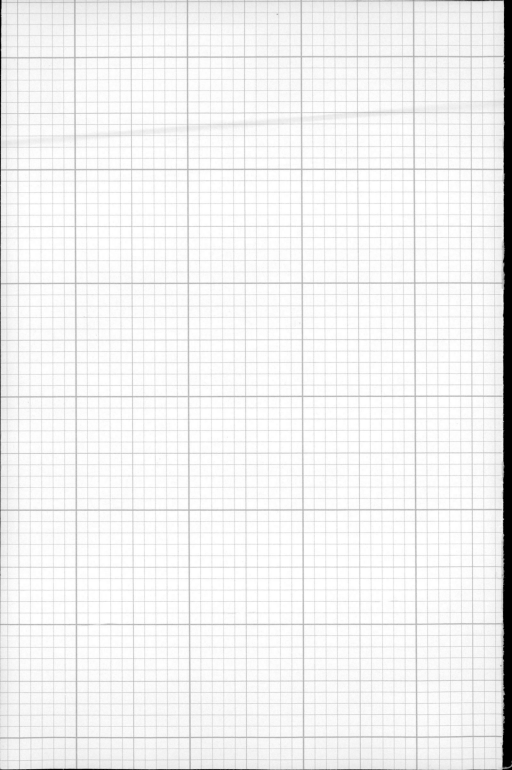

THIS NOTEBOOK BELONGS TO:

Aaron

THE QUESTIONEERS SERIES

THE QUESTIONEERS

AARON SLATER

AND THE SNEAKY SNAKE

by Andrea Beaty

illustrations by David Roberts

AMULET BOOKS

NEW YORK

To our Abrams family. Thank you
for making the world a better place!
—A.B. and D.R.

Cataloging-in-Publication Data has been applied for and may be obtained from the Library of Congress.

ISBN 978-1-4197-5398-5

Text copyright © 2023 Andrea Beaty
Illustrations copyright © 2023 David Roberts
Book design and coloring by Charice Silverman

Published in 2023 by Amulet Books, an imprint of ABRAMS. All rights reserved. No portion of this book may be reproduced, stored in a retrieval system, or transmitted in any form or by any means, mechanical, electronic, photocopying, recording, or otherwise, without written permission from the publisher.

Amulet Books® and Amulet Paperbacks® are registered trademarks of Harry N. Abrams, Inc.

Printed and bound in USA
10 9 8 7 6 5 4 3 2 1

Amulet Books are available at special discounts when purchased in quantity for premiums and promotions as well as fundraising or educational use. Special editions can also be created to specification. For details, contact specialsales@abramsbooks.com or the address below.

ABRAMS The Art of Books
195 Broadway, New York, NY 10007
abramsbooks.com

CHAPTER

*O*nce there was a dragon the color of the sun, who slept in the craggy mountains above the Kingdom. Each day, the people wondered when the Sun Dragon would swoop down upon them with its fiery breath. It had not happened in an age. But such things are remembered from age to age.

There was another dragon, the color of the sea, who slept in the deep waters beyond the shore. Each day, the people wondered if the Sea

Dragon would save them once more. It had not happened in an age. But such things—

WHOMP!

A checkered pillow flopped onto Aaron's face, interrupting his latest story. In a single motion, Aaron pulled it off and flung it back at his brother, who sat laughing in his bed.

WHAP!

The pillow hit its mark and Jacob toppled over, giggling.

Aaron sat up.

"Stop doing that!" he said while karate chopping his right hand into his left palm in the American Sign Language (ASL) sign for STOP!

Aaron and Jacob freely mixed sign language and speech. The whole family took sign language classes with Jacob, who was hard of hearing. The whole family was Mom, Mum, Gabriel, Tracy, Jacob, and Aaron. Their cats, Oberon and Eugene, relied on meowing loudly and cuteness to communicate.

Aaron and Jacob shared a room, which was fine most of the time. Except when Aaron was thinking or drawing or reading or sleeping or . . .

WHOMP!

The pillow hit Aaron again.

"Get up," said Jacob.

"I'm busy," said Aaron. "I'm making up a story."

"Here's a story," said Jacob. "Mum is waiting for you and you are LATE!"

He dramatically flapped his right hand down and back in the sign for LATE.

"Late for wha—" Aaron started, but he instantly remembered. "The zoo!" he said, jumping out of bed.

The Questioneers often helped Zookeeper Fred at the zoo. This week, they were working on Frogville, and Aaron had almost forgotten. He grabbed his sketch pad and ran out of the bedroom, but not before he sent the pillow in a beeline toward his brother's face. Jacob caught the pillow, ready to bean Aaron with it, but it was too late. Aaron was already out of the house and on his way to the zoo.

CHAPTER

Aaron was the first Questioneer to reach the native habitat at the center of the zoo. It used to be a boring concrete pool surrounded by wide gravel paths. Now it was Frogville, a big pond in a garden with benches, curvy paths, and birdhouses. The Questioneers were helping plant native flowers and shrubs to attract pollinators and provide homes for local insects, birds, and especially, frogs.

Zookeeper Fred was very worried about frogs.

Their populations were dropping fast all around the world because of chemicals and climate change. Even in Blue River Creek, fertilizers and weed killers were running off lawns with each rain. The chemicals ran into the stream and hurt the frogs and other animals that lived there. Frogville could give frogs a clean habitat with insects to eat and water that was safe for their tadpoles. And it could show people a new way to use their yards and help nature.

Aaron sat on a bench and sketched a dragonfly. He drew a different animal each time he visited the zoo. Maybe one day, his sketches would hang in the zoo gallery. He hoped so, anyway.

Suddenly, Aaron heard laughter.

"Ha-ha-ha! Cut it out!"

Aaron looked around. A wiggling pair of legs was sticking out of the hydrangea hedge. Aaron

ran to the hedge. The wiggling legs belonged to Zookeeper Fred.

"Hee-hee-help!" yelled Zookeeper Fred.

"Are you okay?" asked Aaron.

"I'm stuck!" cried Zookeeper Fred. "Ha-ha-ha!"

"What's so funny?" asked Aaron.

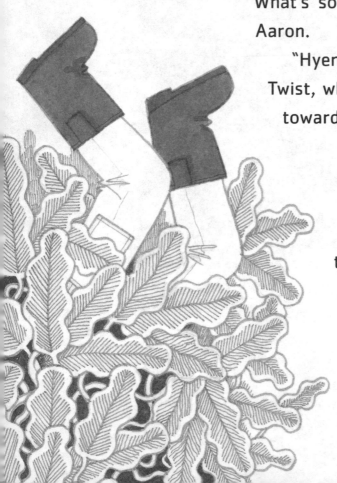

"Hyenas!" called Ada Twist, who was running toward them.

"Hyenas!?!" cried Aaron. "Where!?!"

"Through the hedge," said Ada. "This is the backside of the hyena habitat.

Hyenas give him the tickles every time he sees them."

Aaron peeked through the hedge. Sure enough, two large hyenas with sharp teeth were looking back at him through a wire fence. Their barks sounded like laughter and sent Zookeeper Fred into another fit of giggles.

Hee-hee-hee! Ha-ha-ha!

Just then, Rosie Revere arrived with Iggy Peck and Sofia Valdez. Zookeeper Fred was Rosie's uncle. She looked at his wiggling legs and sighed.

"Did the hyenas get Uncle Fred again?" she asked. "The gardeners planted the hedge to keep that from happening! Stop laughing, Uncle Fred."

"I can't," snorted the zookeeper. "It's just too fun-hee-hee-hee!"

"Think of something sad!" said Aaron.

"Like mushy cereal!" said Sofia.

"Or melted ice cream!" said Ada.

"Or Gothic style windows in an Art Deco mansion," said Iggy, who loved architecture.

The Questioneers looked at Iggy.

"What?" he asked. "It's an architectural nightmare!"

"Iggy's right!" said Uncle Fred. "The wrong windows ruin the whole design."

He stopped laughing. He sniffled. He looked like he might even cry.

"Pull it together, Uncle Fred!" said Rosie.

Zookeeper Fred wiggled and waggled and plopped onto the path. He brushed off his uniform and straightened his mustache.

"Thank you," he said. "I was looking for Vern in the hedge when the hyenas got me laughing."

"Who's Vern?" asked Aaron.

Zookeeper Fred pulled out a photo of a tiny green snake hiding in a sandwich.

"Vern is the sweetest snake I've ever met," he said, brushing away a tear.

Aaron wasn't a big fan of snakes, but he had to admit that a tiny green snake in a sandwich was pretty cute. Unfortunately, not every animal at the zoo was cute. The zoo was filled with big predators with very big teeth and very, VERY big appetites. They would love a little green snack if one slithered by.

Aaron looked at his friends. He could tell he wasn't the only one thinking it. Vern was in danger. And there was nothing funny about that.

CHAPTER

The Questioneers wandered around the zoo, looking for Vern. It didn't take long to realize they had a problem. The zoo had lots of animals, but it had a million times more plants! How could they find a tiny green snake in a giant green jungle? They gave up looking and went to Uncle Fred's office. The zookeeper looked sadly at his lunch.

"Vern loved hiding in sandwiches," he said with a sigh.

"It was kind of a problem," said Rosie. "One time, Uncle Fred thought Vern was a pickle and almost took a bite! I invented some machines to keep Vern out of Uncle Fred's lunch."

Rosie pointed to a shelf of contraptions. Each was labeled **SNAKE-AWAY**, followed by a number. There were seventy-three!

"Did they work?" asked Sofia.

"Not really," said Rosie. "It makes me wonder what scared Vern away this time?"

"Man," said Aaron, "Vern is a sneaky snake." He looked closely at the gizmos. "This one's cool," he said, pointing at the Snake-Away 47. "Is it a trebuchet? Can we try it out?"

The word sounded like *tray-boo-shay*. The machine was a kind of catapult with a long arm on one end and a weight on the other.

"I love a trebuchet!" said Iggy. "You can use them to toss boulders over castle walls!"

"Or junk into the recycling bins!" said Sofia. "C'mon! Let's take out the recycling!"

"Thank you, kids," said Uncle Vern sadly. "We'll work on Frogville tomorrow. I'll go back to hunting for Vern after lunch. I hope he's okay."

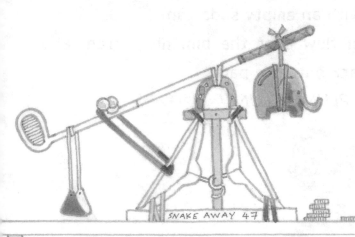

SNAKE AWAY 47

Rosie hugged her uncle. "Vern is a smart snake," she said. "He'll be okay. We'll be outside when you're ready to look some more."

Sofia grabbed the recycling basket and headed out the door to the bins along the path. Aaron grabbed the Snake-Away 47. Iggy, Ada, and Rosie followed them.

Aaron put the trebuchet on the path and Ada loaded it with an empty soda can.

The can flew over the bin, hit a tree, and plopped back onto the path.

SWISH! PLUNK! CLUNK!

"Hmm," said Ada. "Too much force."

"Wrong angle," said Rosie.

Ada and Rosie made some calculations and adjusted the trebuchet for the perfect shot. They loved working together on engineering and science problems.

Sofia reloaded the soda can. Aaron launched the trebuchet and—

SWOOSH!

The can sailed in a smooth arc straight into the bin.

"Woo-hoo!" the Questioneers cheered.

Iggy loaded the next can and Aaron launched it.

SWOOSH!

The Questioneers launched cans, cups, and paper wads into the bin. Each time, they cheered loudly.

A woman with triplets stopped to watch.

Aaron held up a paper coffee cup with a plastic lid.

"The last one," he said, loading it on the trebuchet.

He launched the trebuchet.

SWISH!

POP!

Halfway through the air, the lid popped off the cup and a tiny green head poked out. It was Vern! He wiggled and waggled, sending the cup off course. It bounced off a tree and Vern flew out of the cup.

Up, up he soared!

The triplets clapped.

Down! Down he fell.

The triplets cheered.

PLOP!

Vern landed on a triplet's head.

The triplet squealed with delight.

"I've got a snake hat!" he yelled.

"I want one!" yelled a triplet.

"Me too!" yelled the other one.

"EEEEEEK!" screamed the woman. "A snake! A snake!"

"Yay!" they yelled together. "He's cute!"

"No, he's not!" yelled their mom, running this way and that.

Uncle Fred heard the commotion and ran outside, sandwich in hand.

"Can I help y—" he started. "Vern!" he cried.

Zookeeper Fred ran to the kid wearing Vern,

and Vern saw his chance! He sprang onto Uncle Fred's arm and squeezed into the sandwich.

"EEEEEEK!" the woman shrieked. "That poisonous snake just attacked my son!"

"Vern is not pois—" started Uncle Fred.

"He might have squeezed my boy to death!" she cried.

"Vern is not a boa constrict—" started Uncle Fred.

"Or swallowed him whole!" she cried.

Uncle Fred looked at the rather large kid and the teeny, tiny snake. He squinted, trying to imagine Vern swallowing anything bigger than a bug.

"Could he?" he asked. "I don't think—"

Before he could say anything more, the woman grabbed her kids' hands and ran for the zoo gates.

"Thank you for finding Vern!" Uncle Fred called after her. "I'm sorry he was on your son's head!"

But she was gone.

Fred gently touched Vern's tiny head.

"It's okay, Vern," he said. "The trouble is over."

The Questioneers spent the rest of the afternoon helping Zookeeper Fred in Frogville. They had a lot of fun. What they did not have was a clue. Not even a teeny, tiny, itsy-bitsy clue how wrong Uncle Fred was.

How very, VERY wrong indeed.

CHAPTER

SNAKE-AWAY 47

CHAPTER

The next morning, Aaron was the last one up. His sister, Tracy, was practicing guitar on the window seat when he came into the kitchen. His brothers, Gabriel and Jacob, sat at the table, eating Crunchy Munchy cereal. Aaron's favorite. He poured himself a big bowl and reached for the milk.

It was empty. He shook the carton and looked inside. It was still empty.

Aaron glared at Gabriel.

"EMPTY!" he signed.

Gabriel grinned, crammed a heaping spoon of cereal into his mouth, and chomped as loudly as he could.

CRUNCH. CRUNCH. CRUNCH.

MUNCH. MUNCH. MUNCH.

"This cereal really is crunchy *and* munchy!" Gabriel said with his mouth full of cereal. "And that milk is sooooo good!"

Aaron rolled his eyes.

CRUNCH. CRUNCH. CRUNCH.

MUNCH. MUNCH. MUNCH.

Tracy picked up the beat on her guitar.

STRUM. STRUM. STRUM.

STRUM. STRUM. STRUM.

"YOU SNOOZE, YOU LOSE!" signed Jacob with a grin.

He tapped his fingers on the table.

TAP. TAP. TAP.

TAP. TAP. TAP.

Aaron groaned. He knew what came next.

CRUNCH. CRUNCH. CRUNCH.

STRUM. STRUM. STRUM.

TAP. TAP. TAP.

Tracy closed her eyes, tilted her head, and began to sing. Her voice was smooth and full of emotion.

Aaron's got the blues . . .

STRUM. STRUM. STRUM.

Yeah, he's got the blues . . .

STRUM. STRUM. STRUM.

He's got the

doggone,

milk's gone.

Cereal Blues!

He's got the blues!

STRUM. STRUM.

The Cereal Blues!

STRUM. STRUM.

He's got the

bowl's dry

wanna cry

Cereal Blues . . .

The blues poured out of Tracy and filled the kitchen with music that was sweet and crunchy and soggy and sad all at the same time. Jacob drummed his spoon on the table. Gabriel crunched along in rhythm. Aaron tried to frown, but it was impossible. Some version of the "Breakfast Blues" happened every day at his house. Music was part of a complete balanced breakfast for the Slater family.

The fourth verse of the "Cereal Blues" was in full swing—with Aaron playing the cereal box like a tambourine—when Mom and Mum got home with groceries. Mum plunked a paper bag onto the table and pulled out a carton of milk and a newspaper.

Meanwhile, Mom grabbed two mugs and danced over to the coffee machine. She danced back again and set down the mugs just as Tracy wrapped up the song . . .

Our moms just got back.

STRUM. STRUM. STRUM.

There's milk in the sack.

STRUM. STRUM. STRUM.

It came from a cow

and now you know how

we're gonna end these Cereal Bluuuuuuuueeeeeeeees!

The note hung in the air like perfume. And then it was gone. With a final strum, Tracy stood up and took a bow. Everyone clapped and cheered. Everyone, that is, except Aaron, who sat stone-still, staring at the newspaper.

City Investigates Snake Incident at Zoo

The city is reviewing reports of an incident at the Blue River Creek Zoo involving a snake and a boy. A citizen reported a small, green snake dropping onto the head of her son during a visit. There are no reports of injuries.

The Office of Unexpected Animals is investigating. The office reports to the Blue River Creek Division of Groovy Critters, which oversees the zoo, the aquarium, and that tree in the park where all the pigeons like to hang out.

When asked for comment, Zookeeper Fred said, "I'm sorry that Vern accidentally dropped on the boy's head. Vern is not an outdoor snake and prefers to hide in sandwiches. Though, he did make a good-looking hat."

CHAPTER

The phone rang. Mum answered it.

"Hello, Thomas!" she said. "What? . . . Are you sure? . . . Flying ones? . . . Indeed! . . . Goodbye!"

She hung up the phone.

"What was that?" asked Mom.

"That was Thomas Frost," said Mum. "He says that a flying snake attacked a kid at the zoo yesterday!"

"SNAKE ATTACK?" signed Mom. "I didn't know snakes could fly," she said.

"They can't," said Aaron. "I was there. That's not what happened."

He handed her the newspaper.

"This article doesn't mention flying snakes at all," said Mom.

"Vern can't fly," said Aaron. "He's just a little green snake."

"That's better than a big, flying snake!" said Mum. "It's still scary. Why is the zoo letting the snakes loose? There are kids at the zoo!"

"That was kind of our fault," said Aaron. "I wanted to test Rosie's trebuchet, and Vern was hiding in the recycling and Sofia—"

Aaron's moms looked very confused.

"I'll show you," said Aaron.

He pulled out his sketchbook and began drawing as he told them what had happened at the zoo.

"Rosie made this trebuchet," he said, "but we didn't know that Vern was hiding in the cup. So, when I launched the trebuchet—"

SWOOSH!

Aaron sketched streaks across the picture to show the motion of the coffee cup flying through the air. He added sound effects, too.

SNAP! WHOOOSH! PLOP!

Watching Aaron draw and tell the story was like watching an animated movie. Finally, he reached the end.

". . . he landed on the triplet's head!" exclaimed Aaron. "The kid thought it was awesome, but his mom kind of freaked out."

"I would freak out, too!" said Mum. "Snakes aren't hats!"

"It was an accident," said Aaron. "But now people think it was like a monster movie!" Aaron sketched a giant flying snake devouring the city. "Like this!" he said.

"COOL!" signed Gabriel.

Jacob nodded.

"Well . . ." said Mom, comparing the pictures. "I guess Vern doesn't look too scary."

"He looks like a pickle," said Mum. "But is it safe? Maybe you should avoid the zoo until they sort this thing out."

"But we're supposed to help Uncle Fred

again," said Aaron. "Plus, there's a new panther to sketch."

"We don't know enough about the situation," said Mom.

Aaron looked at his moms. His parents were fair people, but once they made up their minds about something, it was hard to change them. He had to handle this carefully, or he would be spending the day drawing his normal-size cats instead of the big cats at the zoo. Oberon and Eugene were great, but they did not rule the jungle. Just the Slater house.

Aaron thought for a moment. This would take strategy.

"You might be right," he said. "We don't know enough about the situation."

Mom raised her eyebrow.

"Okay . . ." she said suspiciously. "So . . .?"

"So maybe . . ." said Aaron, "maybe we should do that thing you're always telling us to do."

"Pick up your socks?" asked Mom.

"Put away your backpack?" asked Mum.

"No!" said Aaron. "You always say, 'Facts first.' So let's go get some facts."

Mom and Mum looked at each other and smiled.

"Dang," said Mum. "He got us with our own words. I guess we're doing something right."

"Yep," said Mom. "I guess we're going to the zoo."

CHAPTER

The whole family had planned to spend the day at the zoo while Aaron was helping Uncle Fred. Mom wanted to know more first, so she and Aaron left the rest of the family at the aquarium next door.

Mom and Aaron headed toward the zoo office. The zoo was oddly quiet. The paths were usually filled with families and kids in strollers. Today, they were empty.

Where was everyone?

Aaron and Mom followed the winding path. They turned the corner and stopped short. A noisy crowd of people with signs were standing right in front of Zookeeper Fred's office.

"HISS! BOO! NO SNAKES AT THE ZOO!" the crowd chanted.

"Hey!" called a voice.

Aaron looked around. Rosie waved at them from a small path.

"This way," she called. She led them through a side door.

"Good morning, Priyala," said Zookeeper Fred, shaking Mom's hand. "Hi, Aaron! I'm glad you're both here. That yelling outside is scaring Vern. I told them I was sorry. And I asked them to stop yelling, but they just got louder. I don't understand."

"I think they're upset," said Mom.

"They shouldn't be," said Zookeeper Fred. "Vern is fine. I got him a new glass tank to calm him down. See?"

A new glass tank sat on Uncle Fred's desk. It contained a tomato and lettuce sandwich.

"I don't think they're worried FOR Vern," said Aaron. "They're worried ABOUT him. They think he attacked someone."

"Why would Vern do that?" asked Zookeeper Fred. "People are much too big for him to swallow whole. And their hair would tickle his tummy!"

Uncle Fred was missing the point. He loved

Vern so much, he could only see the situation from the snake's point of view. But the people outside were scared. The only information they had was from rumors and the tiny article in the paper. They could only see the situation from their point of view. How could the two sides understand each other?

"Some people are scared of snakes," said Mom, nervously looking at the glass case. "Is he in there?"

"You have to get close to see him," said Zookeeper Fred.

"Oh," said Mom. Reluctantly, she looked closer.

A teeny, tiny green tail stuck out of the sandwich. Mom leaned closer still. Suddenly, a tiny green head popped out of the sandwich and a little black tongue flicked out of the snake's mouth.

"Eek!" Mom cried and jumped back.

Aaron burst out laughing.

"It's not funny," said Mom. Then, despite herself, she laughed, too.

"Well . . ." she said, "it's a little funny. He's teeny tiny, isn't he? And kind of cute . . . for a snake. But is he poisonous? Does he bite? Where did he come from? What does he eat?"

Her fear melted as her curiosity grew. She had lots of questions, and Zookeeper Fred had lots of answers. The more he told her about Vern, the more comfortable she became. Uncle Fred reached into a cardboard box and pulled out a book. He handed it to Aaron.

"I wrote a book about Vern!" said Zookeeper Fred. "Have a copy! I have lots!"

"Vern is very gentle," said Uncle Fred. "He's not interested in you unless you

Know Your **GREEN SNAKE**

- Smooth green snakes are entirely bright green on top. They measure from 11 to 25 inches (30.0–66 cm) long.

- The scientific name of the smooth green snake is *Opheodrys vernalis*.

- They live in grasslands all the way from northeastern Canada to the eastern edge of the Rocky Mountains, from near the Arctic all the way south to Illinois and Virginia.

- The smooth green snake's bright green color helps them hide in meadows, marshes, prairies, and along lakes.

- Smooth green snakes are NOT poisonous.

- They eat insects and sometimes amphibians like frogs. They love to eat grasshoppers, spiders, slugs, and crickets. Who doesn't?

- Like all snakes, they do not chew. They swallow their food whole.

- They are eaten by other snakes, hawks and crows, raccoons, foxes, and other predators. Smooth green snakes help control pest insects.

- However, the smooth green snake's population is declining because of insecticides and habitat loss.

are lunch. But he can tell you're not lunch with his tongue." He pointed at Vern's tiny tongue, which flicked out every second or so. "It has a special organ that senses chemicals in the air. You know," he said, "snakes are more scared of people than people are of snakes."

"I doubt that . . ." said Mom. "People are pretty scared of things they don't understand. Especially when their kids are involved. And that's a fact." She smiled at Aaron. "We'll read your book together," she said, "and see what we learn."

Aaron nodded. "That would be helpful," he said.

Aaron loved reading. He was getting better at it, but he still struggled because of his dyslexia. His parents helped him practice every day. They also shared books as a family. He loved listening to them read in the swing while he sketched chalk pictures on the slate walk in the garden.

Sometimes, he sat in the swing with his family and closed his eyes while stories drifted around him like music. Stories were everything to Aaron.

"I'd like that," he said. "Maybe we—"

RING! RING!

"Hello," said Zookeeper Fred. "Oh no! . . . Oh no! . . . Oh, I see."

Zookeeper Fred sadly hung up the phone. He plopped into his chair and frowned. His mustache drooped.

"What's wrong, Uncle Fred?" asked Rosie.

"That was the mayor," said Zookeeper Fred. "They're closing the zoo!"

CHAPTER

"Closing the zoo?" cried Aaron.

"People complained about Vern!" said Zookeeper Fred. "The city council votes tomorrow to decide what to do!"

"About what?" asked Aaron.

"About the snakes," said Zookeeper Fred. "They want to get rid of the snakes."

"You mean Vern?" asked Rosie.

Zookeeper Fred looked at his niece and blinked back a tear. "No . . ." he said quietly. "All of them."

Rosie gasped. "They can't do that!"

"They can," said Uncle Fred. "The zoo is in the city charter and the council controls the funds. They can take away the snakes if there is a safety issue. They could even close the zoo . . . forever."

"What about the investigation in the article?" asked Aaron.

"It's over," said Zookeeper Fred. "They found that Vern was not a problem and that it was a rare accident. But the city council doesn't know if it should support snakes—or the zoo—if people are scared."

Uncle Fred quietly cleared his throat. "Ahem . . ." he said softly, "well . . . I better get back to work." He stood up and straightened his hat and his mustache.

"Can we help?" asked Rosie.

"Maybe another day," said Uncle Fred.

He hugged Rosie and went out the office door. Rosie, Aaron, and Mom followed him out.

Uncle Fred walked to the protestors.

"I'm sorry Vern got out," he said. "Vern has a new tank now, and it's never going to happen again. But . . . the zoo is closed for now."

"Hurray!" cheered the crowd.

They hoisted their signs and headed toward the zoo exit, chanting as they went: "Hey! Hey! Give a cheer! Those sneaky snakes are outta here! Hey! Hey! . . ."

Uncle Fred grabbed a bucket of feed and headed toward the hyena enclosure. For the first time since he became zookeeper, Fred stood by the hyenas absently tossing out chow. Though the hyenas barked and made faces at him, he did not laugh. He did not chuckle. He did not giggle or hoot or crack a smile.

Rosie looked sadly at her uncle.

"There's something I have to do," Rosie said to Aaron. "I'll meet you at the aquarium in a couple of minutes."

Aaron and Mom met the rest of the Slaters at the aquarium. Rosie joined them a few minutes later. On the walk to Aaron's house, Tracy softly strummed her guitar and sang:

> *We got the blues . . .*
> *We got the blues . . .*

The zoo is shut . . .

It's nuthin' but . . .

the Sneaky Snake Blues . . .

Rosie and Aaron walked silently. They were deep in thought. They had to find a way to save the zoo. They didn't know how, but one thing was for sure: They needed help.

When they stepped into Aaron's yard, that's exactly what they found.

CHAPTER

Rosie called from the zoo," said Sofia. "How can we help?"

Aaron was glad to see them. Facing problems was always easier with friends. He and Rosie told them about the mayor and the protestors at the zoo.

"Uncle Fred says the snakes might have to go," said Rosie. "They might even close the zoo forever! What would Uncle Fred do then? The zoo is *everything* to him!"

Rosie blinked back a tear. Sofia hopped out of the swing and gave her a hug.

"Don't worry! If we built a park," she said, "we can save a zoo!"

Sofia knew that people could change things if they worked together. She had led her friends and neighbors to get a new park in Blue River Creek. Working together could help save the zoo, too.

"I have SOOOOO many questions!" said Ada, pulling out a notebook. "Why does Vern hide in sandwiches? Do snakes eat sandwiches? How do snakes hold sandwiches? What kind of sandwiches do they like best?"

"I have a question, too," said Iggy. "Who thought up the name Parents Stopping Sneaky Snakes Today? PSSST!?! It sounds like something I would say at a movie. PSSST! Pass the popcorn!"

"Here's another one," said Aaron. "If people

get rid of Vern because they don't like him, can they get rid of other animals they don't like, too?"

"I don't like squids," said Iggy. "They're so squiddy. Squiddish? Squiddable? I don't know what you call it, but I don't like them."

"I do," said Sofia. "They're really smart."

"I don't like jellyfish," said Rosie. "They aren't jelly or fish. They're confusing. But I want other people to enjoy them, so I want them to stay in the zoo."

"Aaron's right," said Sofia. "If people start getting rid of animals they don't like, we won't have a zoo at all! At least not one for EVERYBODY to enjoy. We've got to do something."

"Let's brainstorm!" said Ada.

"With chalk!" said Aaron.

He grabbed a bucket of chalk and sat down on the slate walk. It was his favorite place to draw and think. Soon, all the Questioneers were busy drawing and brainstorming ways to save the zoo.

They sketched their ideas on the slate paving stones. When they got a new idea, they moved to a new stone down the path. Before long, a trail of ideas zigzagged through the garden.

The Questioneers had one brainstorming rule: No idea is too weird. A weird idea might not work, but it might spark another idea that sparks another idea that sparks another . . . and THAT idea could lead to an answer! Or maybe just another weird idea. In either case, it's how brainstorming works.

SNAKE ZOO

Snake Rocket

ASTROSNAKE

SNAKE IN SPACE

CHAPTER

Aaron stood back and looked at the trail of ideas. There were some weird ones. There were some wild ones. But were there any good ones?

"We need more time," he said. "If the council listens to PSSSTI, the snakes are doomed!"

"Is that fair?" asked Sofia. "People don't *have* to visit the snakes. But if they get rid of the snakes, I won't get to visit them either. Why should someone else's parents decide if I get to visit snakes?"

"What if I want to become a snake scientist?" asked Ada. "How could I be a herpetologist without snakes to study? We need herpetologists!"

"Why?" asked Iggy.

"Because we need to understand snakes!" said Ada.

"Why?" asked Iggy.

"Because snakes help farmers. They eat mice, which eat their crops," said Ada.

"Why?" asked Iggy. "Oops—I meant to say 'cool!' even though eating mice sounds gross. I think mice are cuter than snakes, but if you have too many of them, I guess they eat all the food. Nature is complicated."

"So are people," said Sofia. "I understand that the people are afraid and they want to protect their kids. But they don't know Vern like we do."

Aaron grabbed Zookeeper Fred's book from the swing.

"That's it!" he cried. "Let's teach them about

Vern! Let's give them the facts and show them there's no danger."

"We'll solve this problem with science!" said Ada. "Let's take Uncle Fred's book to the council so they can read about green snakes! Then they'll want to keep Vern and all the snakes!"

"It's too late," said Iggy. "City Hall is closed for the day. There won't be time in the morning for the whole council to read it."

"Then let's make it easy for them!" said Aaron. "I've got a plan!"

The plan was simple:

1. Make signs with facts from Uncle Fred's book.
2. Take the signs to City Hall at 9:00 AM.
3. Hold up the signs at the windows.
4. The council members read the signs and understand why Vern and all the snakes are important.
5. Council votes to save Vern, the snakes, AND the zoo!
6. Celebrate at Herbert Sherbert's Sherbets.

It had everything a good plan needed. Including sherbet! The Questioneers and Aaron's family got to work. When the signs were done, Rosie, Sofia, Ada, and Iggy headed home.

Things were looking up for Vern and the zoo.

CHAPTER

Aaron lay awake, watching the branches outside his window. Only Oberon's gentle purr broke the midnight silence of the dark house.

Aaron loved the quiet times at night when everyone else was asleep. He could think up stories without anyone interrupting his thoughts. Some nights, he imagined the shadowy branches were the dark forest of an ancient kingdom or the icicle jungle of a distant, frozen planet. Some

nights, there were dragons and mythical beasts and magical flowers. Or robots. Or pirates . . .

Tonight, though, Aaron thought about the plan. He turned it over and over in his mind. This way and that. That way and this. Upside down. Right side up. With each new angle, he tossed and turned and fluffed his pillow. He kicked off his blanket, pulled it up to his chin, then kicked it off again.

Something was not right about their plan. But what? It had all the facts the city council needed to make the right decision: We need snakes. Snakes are important to the ecosystem. Snakes eat pests. Snakes are—

Aaron yawned.

Snakes are . . .

Yaaaawwwwwwn.

Snakes are . . . boring?

Boring? *No,* he thought. *Snakes aren't boring . . . Are they?*

Aaron thought about Vern hiding in a sandwich in Zookeeper Fred's office. Vern was tiny. He was green. He wasn't a venomous cobra or a twenty-foot python hunting a panther in the jungle, but was he boring?

Aaron stretched and readjusted his blanket again.

Vern wasn't boring, even if he ate grasshoppers instead of deadly jungle cats. After all, Vern was sneaky! He could have hidden anywhere in the zoo, and they would never have found him. Then he popped out of a coffee cup! That was so sneaky. And maybe—thought Aaron, closing his eyes and letting out a long, deep yawn—maybe Vern did it on purpose . . .

Maybe . . . Aaron thought . . . *Maybe, Vern wasn't just a green snake. Maybe, he was a master of disguise! A spy! A detective! A reptile who traveled the world looking for adventure, solving mysteries, and eating grasshoppers! And bonbons.*

In that moment, Aaron could see it all! The Adventures of Detective Dangernoodle: International Snake of Mystery! From Paris to Peru . . . Singapore to Seattle. From the Great Wall of China to the tiny paper cup in Uncle Fred's trash can, Vern was on the case.

The Adventures of Detective Dangernoodle unfolded in Aaron's imagination like a movie. With every scene, Aaron's thoughts drifted further and further from the plan . . . and the city council . . . and the zoo . . . and . . . and . . .

Aaron snuggled beneath his blanket as Oberon's purr melted into the gentle rumble of a tiny Vespa carrying a sneaky green snake to his next adventure.

CHAPTER

Aaron was up early the next morning. He was ready by the door with his snake posters before his siblings finished breakfast.

"C'mon," he said, while signing HURRY.

At last, they headed toward City Hall. Sofia was waiting for them by the library. "Iggy got a spot near the door," she said.

"Why?" asked Aaron. "There's lots of room on the landing."

"You'll see," said Sofia.

They turned the corner and Aaron stopped short. Blue River Creek City Hall was a big, impressive building with giant glass doors that opened onto a big landing. Wide steps led from the landing to the plaza below. A chanting crowd filled all the steps and spilled onto the plaza. The landing was roped off, and a podium and city flag stood to the right of the glass doors.

Aaron's heart sank as they got closer. PSSST! signs were everywhere. The people carrying them chanted:

> Hiss! Boo! No snakes at the zoo!
> Hiss! Boo! No snakes at the zoo!

Sofia gave Aaron a reassuring look. "C'mon," she said.

They squeezed through the crowd to the top of the steps, where Ada, Iggy, and Rosie stood with Sofia's grandfather and a few familiar faces. They held their signs high and waved them at the doors of the City Hall in case anyone was watching from inside the building.

Aaron looked at the signs of the other protesters. Only a few supported keeping the snakes in the zoo. Where had all these people come from? Who were they? Had everyone at the zoo brought a crowd of people?

Aaron saw the woman with her triplets. The kids wore funny paper snake hats with googly eyes. They hissed and wiggled and giggled at each other.

"I guess everybody had the same idea," said Iggy.

Aaron frowned. "We should have told everyone we know!"

"It's okay," said Ada. "We don't have as many people, but science is on our side."

Aaron looked down. He was standing on a glossy pamphlet. He picked it up.

Aaron crammed the pamphlet into his pocket. He lifted his sign a little higher and joined his friends in a chant of their own.

Save the snakes!

Save the snakes!

CHAPTER

After a few minutes, the doors opened and the mayor rolled out and waved to the chanting crowd. The city council gathered behind him. They were close enough to read the Questioneers' signs. Aaron and his friends yelled even louder.

Save the snakes!

Save the snakes!

Their chants were swallowed by the roar of the crowd.

Hiss! Boo! No snakes at the zoo!

Hiss! Boo! No snakes at—

SQUEEEEEEEEK!

An ear-piercing squeal blasted from the speakers as the mayor turned on the microphone. The crowd went silent.

"Oops, sorry!" said the mayor. He tapped the microphone.

An ASL interpreter stood to the left of the mayor, signing the mayor's comments as he spoke.

". . . Hello. Hello. Good morning!" said the mayor. "Thank you for sharing your views on the Blue River Creek Zoo."

The crowd chanted again. The mayor raised his hand and they quieted down.

"The city council and I are glad to see so many citizens involved! We will decide using science and what's best for the community." He seemed to look directly at the Questioneers when he said it. Maybe the message had gotten through!

Aaron looked at Ada.

"Science!" she whispered.

Aaron smiled. The mayor continued.

"We want to hear from citizens," he said. "We are holding an emergency meeting in a few minutes. Clerk Clara Clark has a sign-up list. Speakers on the list will get a numbered ticket and will have three minutes to explain their position.

"We will announce our decision tomorrow afternoon at the Dahlia Festival," he said, "since most of the town will be there anyway!"

The Dahlia Festival was a big deal in Blue River Creek. The gardening club made sure the dahlia beds in Citizens' Park were perfect. The mayor and half of the city council members were in the club. They were keen gardeners and spent their lunch breaks tending the gardens. The Dahlia Festival was a chance for them to show off the flowers and for everyone to celebrate Citizens' Park. Also, there was free ice cream, so everyone in town showed up.

"Thank you!" the mayor said, waving to the crowd.

And with that, he led the city council back through the big glass doors and was gone.

CHAPTER

aron's siblings headed home, but the Questioneers stood together on the landing.

"A list!?!" cried Ada. "How do we find Clerk Clark?"

"I don't see her anywhere," said Rosie.

"Maybe Sofi—" said Aaron.

He looked around. Sofia was gone.

"There she is!" cried Iggy, pointing at a line forming by the glass doors.

They ran to Sofia.

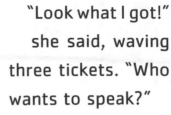

"Look what I got!" she said, waving three tickets. "Who wants to speak?"

"Not me," said Iggy. "Unless it's about Gothic architecture!"

"Ada knows the science best and Rosie knows the zoo best," said Aaron. "And you know the city council best, Sofia."

"But you—" Sofia began.

Suddenly, the doors swung open and the crowd pushed into City Hall, sweeping the Questioneers along with them.

CHAPTER

Aaron and Iggy sat near the back of the room. Ada, Rosie, and Sofia lined up with the other number holders. Clerk Clara Clark called the meeting to order. The ASL interpreter stood next to her.

The first speaker was Thomas Frost.

"I am the president of PSSST!, which stands for Parents Stopping Sneaky Snakes Today," he said. "PSSST! wants to stop flying snakes from attacking our children! It's all in our pamphlet!"

He waved a glossy pamphlet like Aaron had found. Several people cheered.

"Order!" said Clerk Clark.

The crowd quieted and Mr. Frost continued.

"I'm just asking a question here," he said, "but what if flying snakes swallowed all our children? Then we'd have a lot of fat snakes but no kids. That would be bad."

The crowd booed.

"Order!" cried the clerk.

The crowd hushed.

Next was a woman in a "BOO to the ZOO" T-shirt.

"We should not have wild animals at the zoo,"

she said. "They're dangerous and scary. And one time, a monkey made faces at me. That was rude. And Zookeeper Fred is not good at his job."

Next, it was Rosie's turn. The woman's words about her Uncle Fred had stung. Rosie's cheeks were bright red, and she felt hot. She instantly forgot everything she had planned to say. She looked around nervously.

"Um . . ." she said. ". . . I'm Rosie . . ."

Rosie looked at her friends, who smiled back. She stood a little taller.

". . . I'm Rosie Revere," she said again, "and Zookeeper Fred is my uncle.

"He's a great uncle," she said. "And he's a great zookeeper. And he didn't mean for Vern to get outside.

"I'm an engineer," she continued. "It takes lots of tries to build an invention, because things go wrong. That's just the process. Things go wrong everywhere. Even the zoo. Well . . . anyway . . . Uncle Fred fixed the problem, so Vern won't get outside again and—"

The next speaker approached the mic. Rosie's time was up, and she hadn't told them how important snakes were.

She sighed.

"Thank you," she said quietly.

She walked to the back of the room and plopped onto the bench next to Aaron.

"It's okay," he whispered.

"I don't think so," said Rosie.

Next, a man complained about a pothole on Baker Street. Then, it was Ada's turn. She held up Uncle Fred's book. She had lots to say but very little time. So she spoke very quickly.

"I'm Ada Twist!" she said. "I'm a scientist, and

I love snakes. Here's a book you should read!"

She took a deep breath and continued.

"Snakes have between 180 and 400 bones in their spines so they can wiggle like this," she said.

Ada wiggled like a snake.

"I only have thirty bones in my spine," she added. "But I can wiggle, too. Snakes are reptiles. They swallow their food whole. They can't even chew. So, a snake isn't going to eat you unless it can swallow you."

She took another deep breath and zoomed on.

"A giant python in a swamp could eat you," she said. "Some of them are twenty feet long and fat as a telephone pole! They can eat a whole deer or a great big alligator! Can you imagine that? I can!"

The audience gasped.

"Don't worry," said Ada. "The zoo isn't a swamp, and Vern is tiny. Now you know about snakes. Thank you!"

She waved goodbye and headed for the seats.

"Oh!" she cried. "I almost forgot. Snakes can't fly!"

With that, Ada plopped onto the bench by Rosie and took a deep breath.

"Phew!" she said. "Problem solved!"

CHAPTER

The problem wasn't solved.

The next two speakers talked about flying snakes terrorizing the zoo and taking over the city. Ada frowned.

"I told them snakes can't fly," she whispered. "Didn't they listen?"

Aaron pointed to a page of the PSSST! pamphlet.

"They just repeated this," he said.

Sofia stepped up to the mic and adjusted her

barrettes. She seemed cool as a cucumber. She glanced at some notes she had written. Then she began.

"Thank you for your hard work on the city council," she said calmly.

"I love Blue River Creek," she said. "I love our public library, our public park, our public school, and our public zoo. Citizens' taxes pay for them. They belong to ALL our citizens. Not just me. Not just you. Not just the members of PSSST! All of us. That's what *public* means."

She continued. "If I built a *private* zoo," she said. "I would only have turtles, because I love them best. My zoo would have great architecture, so Iggy might like it, too.

"However," she said, "my zoo would not be good for Rosie, who loves birds. Or Aaron, who loves big cats. It would be very bad for Ada! She's a scientist and needs to study ALL animals. Including snakes.

"A private, turtle-only zoo would be fine if I

paid for it with *my own money.*" Sofia said. "But the Blue River Creek Zoo is a *public* zoo. It's OUR zoo.

"It's paid for by *ALL* of us," she said. "And it should serve *ALL* of us. Thank you."

The Questioneers cheered. A few people around the audience applauded.

"Order," said Clerk Clark.

Sofia smiled shyly and walked to the back of the room. She squeezed onto the bench next to Ada, who noticed that although Sofia seemed very brave, her hand trembled. Ada squeezed her friend's hand and gave her a big hug.

"You were amazing," Ada whispered.

After that, Sofia's hand didn't tremble at all.

CHAPTER

The meeting continued. Some speakers were for snakes. Some were against. Someone asked for a cracker kiosk next to the cheese kiosk in the park. Everyone cheered for that. Even the clerk.

At last, the line dwindled.

The woman from the zoo stepped up to the mic. She clutched her kids' hands tightly.

"Where's the funny green snake?" asked one triplet. "We like him!"

"We're snakes, too," said another triplet.

"Hisssssss!!!!!!" they said together.

Their snake hats wobbled and bobbled. The snakes' googly eyes swirled around and around. Everyone laughed.

"Order!" said the clerk, trying to keep a straight face.

"My name is Sarah Hartman," said the woman. "I am very upset. We went to the zoo and a snake landed on my son's head. It was very scary."

"I liked it," said the triplet.

"I did not," said Ms. Hartman. "I love the zoo. I'm glad that Zookeeper Fred apologized. But it's not too much to ask for the zoo to be safe for everyone. Thank you."

The last speaker approached the mic. It was Sofia's grandfather.

"Two things can be true at the same time," said Abuelo. "Ms. Hartman and Sofia are both right. The zoo should be safe, and it should serve all the people.

"When scary things happen, we react from fear," he said. "But if we get rid of things—like the snakes—because we don't understand them, we lose something important. We lose the chance to learn what they can teach us. Snakes are very different from us. They have their own beauty and deserve to exist and be appreciated as they are. And they can also help us."

Abuelo looked at the Questioneers seated together. When he turned back to the microphone, his voice was somber. He gently touched his hand to his heart.

"I am old," he said, "but my Sofia and her friends are young. The future is a beautiful and scary place full of adventures and challenges. We don't know what problems our kids will face in the future or what tools they will need.

"Maybe they'll cure a terrible disease by researching snake cells," he said. "Or engineer a new kind of transportation from studying how snakes move. Or build great buildings with roof tiles like snake scales. Or make wonderful art inspired by the curves of a snake. If we get rid of the snakes, how will our kids do those things? What will we lose if we get rid of the snakes?

"Two things can be true at the same time," he repeated. "We can keep our kids safe *and* help them understand the world so they can face the wonderful and complicated future that awaits them."

CHAPTER

Finally, the meeting ended. The Questioneers burst into the sunshine of the City Hall landing.

"Over here!" cried Mum.

She and Mom stood by a stack of boxes. The boxes were filled with copies of Uncle Fred's book! Gabriel and Tracy were handing out books to people leaving City Hall.

"Jacob told us about the meeting," said Mom, "so we called Uncle Fred. He was too sad to come speak, but he asked us to share his books, so here we are!"

"HELP ME!" signed Jacob.

"O-K," signed Aaron.

Jacob handed Aaron a pile of books. Rosie, Ada, Iggy, and Sofia grabbed some, too. Even Abuelo joined them. They spread out over the landing, handing copies of the book to anyone who would take one. Soon, the crowd was gone and the boxes were empty. Abuelo, the Questioneers, and Aaron's family stood together by the great glass doors.

"I've been to a lot of city council meetings in my life," said Abuelo, "and I've learned two things."

"What are they?" asked Aaron.

"First," said Abuelo, "it's never over until you quit."

"You sound like Great-Great-Aunt Rose!" said Rosie.

"She's a wise woman," said Abuelo.

"What's the other thing, Abuelo?" asked Sofia.

"The other thing," he said, "is that public speaking makes me hungry! Who wants sherbet?"

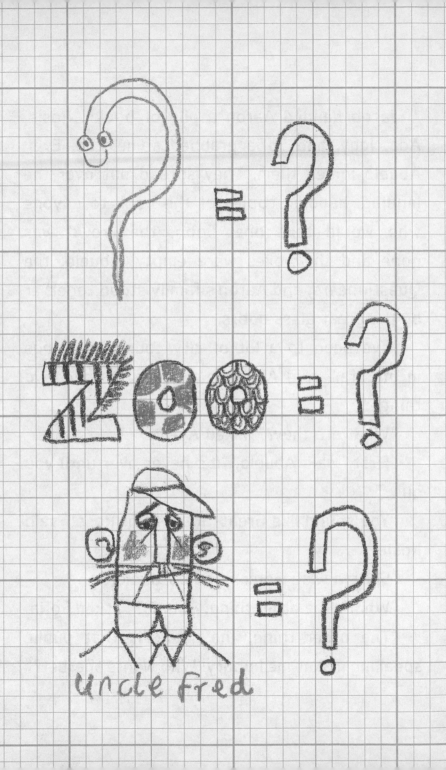

uncle fred

CHAPTER

The Questioneers scooted into their favorite booth at Herbert Sherbert's Sherbets. They ate and talked about the meeting. They all had mixed feelings. Had it gone well? Had it gone badly? How would the council vote? What would happen to the snakes? To the zoo? To Uncle Fred?

"I thought everybody understood," said Ada. "But now I don't know."

"We needed more people," said Rosie. "So

many people who were against the zoo showed up. Why didn't more people show up to support the zoo?"

"I think people are busy," said Iggy. "They don't think about snakes at all. I don't. I think about architecture."

"If people don't care," said Sofia, "we have to help them care! What happens at the zoo affects everyone in the town, even if they don't know it."

"We showed the facts," said Ada. "What more do people need?" She looked at Aaron's sketchbook. He had been doodling while the others talked.

"What do you think, Aaron?" asked Ada.

"I think sometimes, people decide because of their feelings," he said. "Those triplets sure liked snakes, even if their mom was scared. Facts are for their heads, but maybe they need something for their hearts, too."

"So . . ." said Ada, "how do we give people facts *and* make them feel good about snakes?"

"*And* how do we do it in one day?" asked Iggy.

Aaron looked at his sketchbook again.

Suddenly, he grinned. He knew exactly what to do. AND—even better—he knew how to do it!

He popped out of the booth and headed toward the counter.

"Where are you going?" asked Sofia.

"To get us more sherbet," said Aaron. "And then, I'm going to tell you all a story!"

DANGER
Noodle!

CHAPTER

Aaron finished the last bite of sherbet and plunked his spoon into the glass dish. He flipped to a new page of his sketchbook and began drawing. Then, he began to speak . . .

Once upon a time, there was a snake. A snake who was so smart. So clever. So sneaky, that he was a world-famous detective. One time, Detective Dangernoodle battled evil cockroaches from space who had invaded the zoo . . .

The Questioneers were spellbound. Aaron's

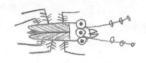

story had everything: Adventure! Science! Mystery! Evil cockroaches from space!

Finally, Aaron reached the end of the story. "And that," he said, "is how we save Blue River Creek Zoo!"

"Don't you mean 'That's how Detective Dangernoodle saved *his* zoo'?" asked Sofia. "We don't have evil alien cockroaches. Do we?"

"I hope not!" said Iggy.

"I wonder what species they are," said Ada.

"I love your story, Aaron," said Rosie, "but it's just a story. Maybe we can invent something instead."

"Let me ask you a question," said Aaron. "Why did you invent the cheese-copter for Great-Great-Aunt Rose?"

"Because I wanted to help her," said Rosie.

"Why?" asked Aaron.

"Because she wanted to fly," said Rosie.

"How did you know?" asked Aaron.

"Ohhhhhhh," said Rosie. "Her stories about flying inspired me!"

"Stories are POWERFUL!" said Aaron. "They can inspire us to make inventions, and they can inspire us to do other things, too!"

"Like learn about things that scare us?" asked Rosie.

"Like snakes?" asked Ada.

"Exactly!" said Aaron. "I listen to lots of books with my family," he said. "If I like the characters, I feel like they're my friends and I want to know more about them."

"Do they make you feel braver?" asked Sofia.

Aaron nodded.

"Detective Dangernoodle could be like a mascot for the zoo!" said Rosie. "Kids will love it!"

"What about their parents?" asked Sofia.

"And the city council and mayor?" asked Ada. "Do you think a story will change their minds?"

"It might!" said Aaron. "But storytelling is just one type of art. All types of art are powerful."

Aaron flipped through his sketchbook.

"I drew this because I was sad one day," he said. "I use art to let my feelings out. But art works in both directions. If I look at art or listen to it, I take it *into* my heart and *into* my mind. Art changes how I feel and think!"

"So we're going to use some art to change their minds?" asked Ada.

"Not quite," said Aaron with a smile. "We're not going to use *some* art . . ." he said. "We're going to use *ALL* of it!"

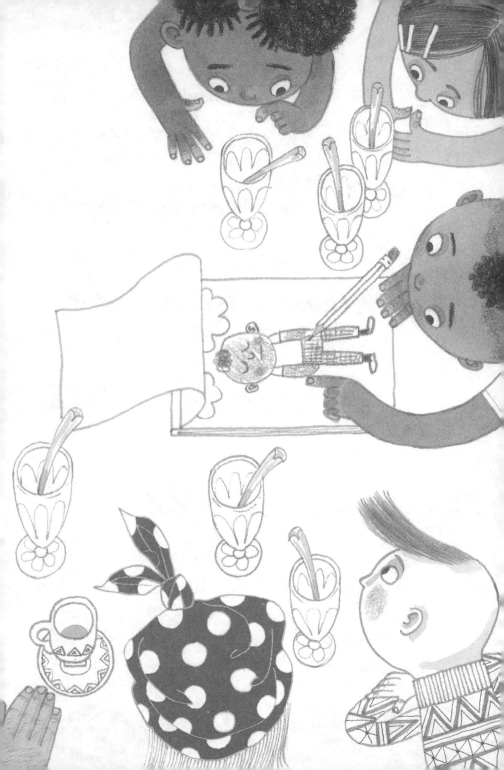

CHAPTER

Once more, the Questioneers brainstormed. They made lists, lists, and more lists! They had so much to do and so little time to do it. They were going to use every kind of art they could to save the zoo. Of course, they would include science and engineering and architecture, too!

They had people. They had a plan. They had a poster!

But would it be enough?

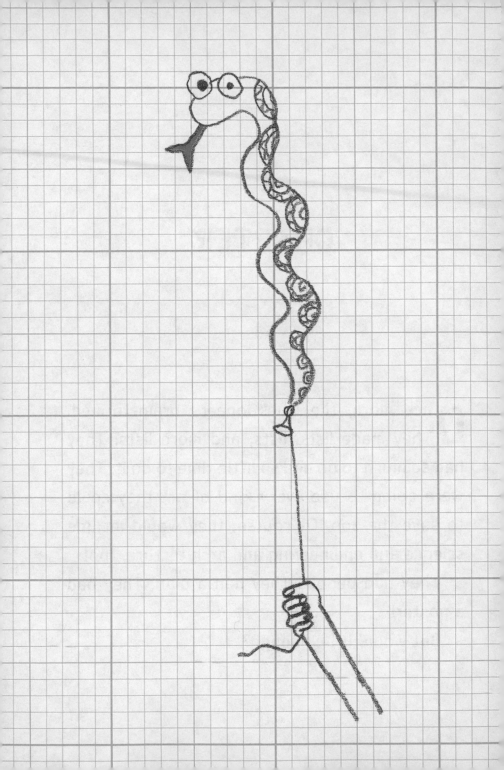

CHAPTER

The Questioneers stood beneath a snake balloon arch and looked at the giant crowd of people waiting to enter. There were people from all over Blue River Creek. Some had been at the city council meeting. A crowd of twenty PSSST! members stood behind a banner that read: **NO SNAKES AT THE ZOO OR THE BLUE RIVER CREEK DAHLIA FESTIVAL OR ANYWHERE IN THIS TOWN!** It was a big banner. And it looked heavy.

A busload of gardeners from Plantsburg stood in the back, chatting about their dahlias.

Snakes can unhinge their jaws and swallow prey three times as wide as their heads!

"The voles devoured my tubers this year," said one gardener.

"The slugs ate mine!" said another. "I hope Blue River Creek's garden did better. It's always so beautiful."

Ms. Hartman pushed through the crowd. She was holding a box of paper snake hats with googly eyes. She was followed by her triplets.

"We made these for you," she said, handing Aaron the box. "I still don't like snakes, but we read the book and maybe snakes are okay, as long as they aren't loose in the zoo. And can't fly."

"I wish they did!" said one triplet.

"Me too!" said another.

"Me three!" said the third one.

The triplets spread their arms out like wings and ran

116

off with Ms. Hartman chasing behind them.

"These are great!" said Sofia, taking the box from Aaron.

"I think we're ready!" said Aaron.

Rosie, Iggy, and Ada ran to their stations in the park. Aaron turned to the crowd.

"Welcome to the First Ever Detective Dangernoodle and Dahlia Festival!" he said. "Meet Vern! Is he scary? Is he wiggly? Is he green? Is he a detective? Come see for yourself!"

Most of the crowd was nervous, but also curious. They cautiously stepped through the arch and headed down the path. The PSSST! group followed them into the festival, carrying their banner and chanting, "No snakes!"

Extreme fear of snakes is called ophidiophobia.

Snakes don't blink. They don't have eyelids. They have clear scales called brilles that protect their eyes.

Humans shed millions of skin cells every day! Snakes shed their skins in one piece. The process is called ecdysis. It happens four to twelve times a year.

Sofia and Abuelo handed out fresh-baked cookies and snake hats to all who wanted them.

"Dangernoodle Snickerdoodles!" said Sofia, waving a cookie in the air.

"They're sssssssssssssuperb!" said Abuelo.

The smell of cinnamon filled the air, and the crowd relaxed as they munched cookies and headed down the path. Every few feet, they passed a sign created by Ada and her family.

Everyone the Questioneers had asked for help had come through.

The Riveters brought their truck for a bandstand, and they were jamming. Tracy played guitar and Jacob

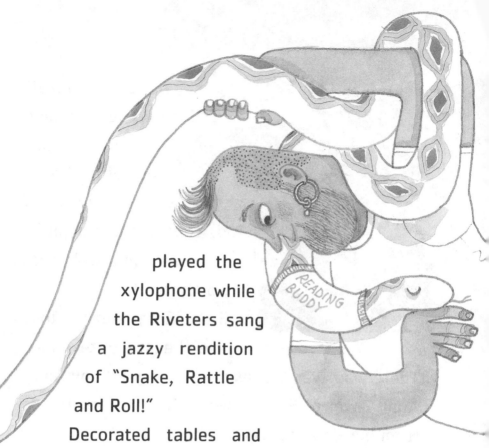

played the
xylophone while
the Riveters sang
a jazzy rendition
of "Snake, Rattle
and Roll!"

Decorated tables and
performance stages lined the path as it wound
through the park toward the dahlia garden. Aaron's
moms did face painting. Further down, Bee and
Beau, who volunteered at the library, introduced
the newest Reading Buddy, William Snakespeare.

Ada's brother, Arthur, performed magic tricks
beneath an oak tree.

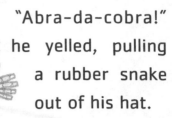

"Abra-da-cobra!" he yelled, pulling a rubber snake out of his hat.

A bunch of kids squealed in delight.

There was a trebuchet workshop led by Rosie. Great-Great-Aunt Rose gave cheese-copter rides. There was even a snake hisssstory talk by Ada's Aunt Bernice. She showed off snake skeletons from her Can You Dig It? shop.

Before long, the festival was in full swing. The crowd was dancing, singing, making art, watching puppet shows, and having fun. Even a few of the PSSST! crowd peeled away from their group and joined the concert. Everything was going perfectly. And everyone was there!

Except the people who mattered the most.

CHAPTER

W here's the mayor?" asked Aaron.

Sofia looked around. "I don't know," she said. "But here's Clerk Clark."

"Oh my!" cried the clerk. "Look what you all did! This is amazing!"

"Where's the city council?" asked Sofia.

"On their way," said the clerk. "They just finished voting."

"What did they decide?" Aaron asked nervously.

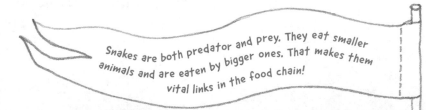

Snakes are both predator and prey. They eat smaller animals and are eaten by bigger ones. That makes them vital links in the food chain!

Clerk Clark didn't have to answer. Her face told the story.

"Oh no!" cried Sofia.

Just then, the mayor and the six city council members arrived. They stared at the snake arch. Three of them frowned at it. Three were delighted. The mayor also frowned. Clearly, the snakes had lost four votes to three.

The three smiling council members grabbed cookies from Sofia's basket and headed into the festival.

"I told them that snakes could be

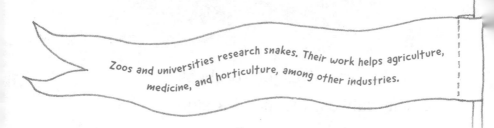

Zoos and universities research snakes. Their work helps agriculture, medicine, and horticulture, among other industries.

fun!" said one of the council members as they walked down the path.

The mayor rolled through the arch, followed by the three frowning council members.

"Cookie?" asked Abuelo.

"Thank you," said the mayor. "You make the best cookies in town."

The mayor and Abuelo had met many times and were sometimes on the opposite side of issues, but they treated each other kindly.

Small snakes eat insects, grubs, and slugs.

Larger snakes eat gophers, mice, and voles.

Slugs and voles eat dahlias!

The mayor chomped on the cookie.

"Delicious as always," said the mayor. "But we must move on. I have a speech to make, and I've got to check on the dahlias. I trapped a slug in the patch last night. They do such damage!"

The mayor and council members headed into the festival, munching cookies as they went.

"Have fun!" called Abuelo.

Then he winked at Aaron and Sofia.

"Remember," he whispered, "it's never over until you quit!"

CHAPTER 24

Sofia, Aaron, and Clerk Clark accompanied the mayor and council members through the festival. They might have started with frowns, but quickly they relaxed and started to enjoy the festival. They passed the music stage. Tracy was performing "Sneaky Snake Blues" and everyone was clapping along.

They passed the comedy stage, where the public librarian, Mr. Page, was telling jokes.

"What do you call a snake who builds things?" he asked. "A boa constructor!"

A council member snickered.

"What do you call a snake who works in government?" asked Mr. Page. "A civil serpent!"

The council member doubled over in laughter and motioned to the mayor to move on without her. "I'll catch up with you," she wheezed. "I love snake jokes!"

She plopped onto the grass and howled for more.

"Ooh!" said another council member. "Balloon art!?!"

They ran toward Rosie's Uncle Ned, who was teaching balloon sculpture.

Clerk Clark went to play a board game called Snakes & Adders. And the last council member joined a conga line of Plantsburg gardeners.

"Humph," said the mayor. "Guess I'll do the speech alone."

"We'll come along," said Aaron.

Aaron, Sofia, and Rosie followed the mayor

toward the dahlia beds. They followed a curve in the path and came to a dense tunnel of dark silky ribbons dangling from overhanging branches.

Suddenly, two giant wiggly snakes jumped onto the path and blocked their way.

"Stop!" they cried. "You're about to see something amazing!"

CHAPTER

The snakes wiggled. They giggled. Their hats fell off.

"Hi, Mr. Mayor," said Ada. "It's just us!"

"I know," said the mayor.

"Are you ready to see something amazing?" asked Iggy.

Iggy led them into the tunnel. The silky streamers brushed against their faces in the dim light. The ribbons were soft and cool. Then, just as the group's eyes adjusted to the dim light in

the tunnel, they burst into the sunshine of the dahlia garden.

It was a stunning explosion of orange! Every shade of orange glowed in the sunshine. There were orange dahlias everywhere! Some were big and spiky. Some were small and round. The air buzzed with bees. Butterflies flitted from flower to flower. The garden was perfect.

"Isn't it amazing?" asked Ada.

The mayor was speechless. He had helped plant the garden. He took care of it every day. But somehow, coming through the dark tunnel into the bright garden was a whole new experience. It was as if he was seeing it for the first time. Looking at it in a whole new way.

He sat silently for a moment.

"I . . ." he said. "I thought you were going to show me the snake."

"He's in the back corner with Uncle Fred," said Rosie. "I'll take you there if you like."

"Thank you," said the mayor. "I think I want to sit here for a minute. I'm . . . well . . . I'm a little overwhelmed."

"Art can do that sometimes," said Aaron.

The Questioneers turned to leave.

"You know," said Sofia. "Blue River Creek has a great public garden."

The mayor smiled and nodded.

"You know," he said, "Blue River Creek has a lot of great public places. And a great public!"

CHAPTER

The mayor sat by the orange dahlias for a long time. Finally, he rolled down the path to the back corner of the garden, where Uncle Fred sat by a large sandwich-shaped structure with a window on one side. It was Vern's vacation house, which had been specially designed by Blue River Creek's most famous architect, Iggy Peck.

A stream of visitors peeked into Vern's window. They oohed and aahed at the small green snake resting on a lettuce bed. They asked Uncle Fred all kinds of questions. They came to see the Snake That Attacked the City or the daring Detective Dangernoodle. They left happy to know Vern, the little smooth green snake from Blue River Creek Zoo. Eventually they wandered off to enjoy the dahlias and get a scoop of SSSSSStrawberry SSSSSSorbet donated by Herbert Sherbert's Sherbets.

Uncle Fred picked up Vern and showed him to the mayor. The mayor looked at Vern. "He's tiny," he said.

"Very," said Uncle Fred. "I think he's quite beautiful."

"Hmm," said the mayor. "Does he really eat slugs?"

"He loves them!" said Uncle Fred.

"Hmm," said the mayor. "I picked a slug off my favorite dahlia, Ivanetti, this morning. They do some damage."

"They do indeed!" said Uncle Fred. "I can't keep them off my Bluest-Blues this year!"

And with that, the mayor and the zookeeper of Blue River Creek discovered that they had something unexpected in common. They talked for hours about dahlias and gardening and slugs and snakes and the zoo and the good people of their town. Especially the kids who cared so much about what happened there.

"Oh my! Look at the time!" said the mayor. "That speech isn't going to give itself!"

While the mayor and Zookeeper Fred had been talking, the festival activities had ended, and everyone had made their way through the ribbon tunnel to the dahlia garden. The crowd cheerfully chatted about the day's events and admired the dahlias, which glowed with a new

intensity in the fading afternoon light. Mr. Frost awkwardly held the folded-up PSSST! banner by himself. His group had evaporated somewhere between the puppet show and the sculpture-making station.

The mayor and city council members headed to the gazebo at the center of the garden, where a microphone had been set up. They chatted as they waited for the crowd to gather around. At last, Clerk Clark introduced them.

The crowd clapped and cheered.

"We live in a marvelous town," said the mayor. "I am honored to be your mayor. I hope you have all enjoyed the beautiful dahlias. I think it's the best display we've ever had."

The Plantsburg gardeners clapped.

"We'll come again next year!" one gardener yelled. "With three buses!"

"Much better than Flowerton's festival!" cried another gardener.

The mayor beamed. The crowd cheered again. The mayor cleared his throat and continued.

"I know that many of you are here today because of the situation at the zoo," he said. "I must tell you that today, the council voted to get rid of the snakes at Blue River Creek Zoo."

The crowd sighed. Mr. Frost and a couple of others cheered.

"But—" started the Questioneers.

"But . . ." the mayor continued, "then we came here to the First Ever Detective Dangernoodle and Dahlia Festival and we changed our minds! We just voted again. We are keeping Vern and the other snakes at the zoo as long as they are safely contained in appropriate enclosures. I learned some new things here today about snakes and why they are important to the zoo and our gardens! Can you believe they eat slugs?"

The Plantsburg gardeners cheered very loudly.

The mayor continued, "I also learned some

things about our town and the people who live here. Thanks to Vern, I've even made a new friend today."

He waved at Zookeeper Fred, who waved back.

The crowd cheered yet again.

"We have a great public," said the mayor, looking at the Questioneers. "And the zoo needs to reflect that and be a great resource for *ALL* our citizens. AND the animals. So, I hope to see you all back here next year at the Second Ever Detective Dangernoodle and Dahlia Festival!"

And with that, the festival was over, though it took a very long time for the conga line to snake all the way back to the big balloon arch. And nobody minded at all.

CHAPTER

It was night, and the Slater house was quiet once more. Oberon and Eugene purred softly at the foot of Jacob's bed. Aaron lay awake, watching the scraggly tree branches dance in the moonlight outside his window. He wanted to sleep, but so much had happened in the last two days and his brain couldn't settle down.

The wind rustled the branches outside the window. Aaron kicked off his covers and fluffed his pillow. He yawned and pulled his covers back up, but nothing helped. He was about to get some water when Jacob flipped on the lamp between their beds.

"I CAN'T SLEEP," signed Jacob.

"SAME," signed Aaron.

They signed back and forth about Vern and the zoo. About how art had saved the day. And how science did, too. And about the festival and what might happen next year at the Second Ever Detective Dangernoodle and Dahlia Festival.

After a few minutes, they grew still.

"AARON," Jacob signed, "WILL YOU TELL ME A STORY?"

"O-K," signed Aaron. "ONCE, THERE WAS A SNAKE—"

Jacob shook his head. "NO," he signed. "THE ONE WITH DRAGONS."

"I DON'T KNOW HOW IT ENDS," signed Aaron.

"YOU'LL FIGURE IT OUT," signed Jacob, pulling his bear close and snuggling into his pillow. "YOU ALWAYS DO."

Aaron smiled at his brother. He took a breath, closed his eyes, and thought a moment. Then, he opened his eyes, raised his hands, and began to paint the story in the air with signs . . .

. . . *ONCE* . . .

He began.

. . . *ONCE THERE WAS A DRAGON THE COLOR OF THE SUN* . . .

THE PARADISE
FLYING SNAKE

We all know that snakes can't fly.
But there's one snake that loves to try.
It spreads its ribcage double wide.
And man, oh man! Just watch it glide
from way up in the canopy
to catch a lizard in a tree,
sitting there so warm and fat
and lunch is over
just
like
that.

It's true that snakes can't fly like birds or bees or bats. But there is one snake that glides from tree to tree in the jungle. The paradise flying snake (*Chrysopelea paradisi*) lives in the high canopy of trees in the dense jungles of Indonesia. It grows to about four feet long. It eats lizards, frogs, and birds.

When it spies its prey, it uses its very strong muscles to extend its body into the air. It holds onto the branch with just the end of its tail. It spreads its ribs and flattens its body to twice its usual width. Then it leaps out and slithers through the air toward its prey. It can glide up to eighty feet away.

Imagine holding on to a branch with your toes and leaping out to catch a frog two houses away! That's some snake!

FROGVILLE

Frogs are amphibians. They spend the beginning of their lives in water, breathing through gills. As adults, they live on land, breathing through lungs. Frogs can also absorb oxygen through their skin. Because of this, they are very sensitive to chemicals such as fertilizers and weed killers, which run into the waterways from lawns, farmland, and roads.

Because frogs are so sensitive to the environment, they are considered "bioindicators" of an ecosystem. Their populations are the first to show trouble signs. Frogs are eaten by predators up the food chain such as snakes, coyotes, hawks, and herons. If frog populations drop, these species can also be in trouble. Without frogs, insect populations can get out of whack. Frogs are also vulnerable to habitat loss, climate change, and disease.

Frogs have been on Earth for more than 200 million years! However, their numbers are declining. More than 500 species of frogs are critically endangered and at risk of extinction!

Zookeeper Fred and the Questioneers are creating a new habitat at the zoo for native frogs and other wildlife. "Native" means they come from the local area.

Like all animals, frogs need food, shelter, and water. Frogville provides all three. Its pond gives frogs a place to lay eggs and tadpoles a place to grow into adult frogs. The garden offers a hiding place for frogs and other animals. The plants offer food for insects, pollinators, and birds.

There are many ways people can follow Frogville's example to help frogs and other wildlife:

- Stop using chemicals on lawns and gardens. That means no chemical fertilizers or weed killers.
- Use a mulching mower to return grass clippings to the lawn. Grass clippings rot and feed the lawn.

- Replace lawn with clover or flowering plant alternatives, which will attract pollinators and are drought-resistant. Saving water also helps the environment!
- Grow native plants. They will attract local insects, which will attract local frogs and other wildlife.
- Use compost and natural plant foods such as liquid seaweed to feed plants if needed.
- Create a water feature. A pond is great, but even birdbaths can help wildlife.
- Even a few flowerpots with flowers can help feed pollinators, which help the rest of the ecosystem. Plus, they are beautiful!

Everyone can help save the frogs!
Ribbit!

WHAT IS BEHIND
JACOB'S EAR?

Aaron's brother, Jacob, is hard of hearing and wears a cochlear implant. It is a device with two parts that help Jacob process sounds. Part of the cochlear implant sits behind Jacob's ear with a microphone that picks up sounds. The sounds are transmitted to the internal part of the implant, which is under the skin behind his ear. The internal part of the device has a small wire that stimulates the nerves inside the inner ear and produces a hearing sensation in Jacob's brain.

WHAT IS ASL?

The Slater family is learning American Sign Language (ASL) so Jacob can communicate how he prefers. ASL is a complete language with its own grammar, vocabulary, and rules for sentence structure. ASL combines hand, face, and body motions.

ASL is one of about 300 natural sign languages used by deaf and hard-of-hearing people around the world. It is used in America and Canada and parts of Africa and Asia. Other sign languages include British Sign Language (BSL), Irish Sign Language (ISL), Chinese Sign Language (CSL), Lange des Signes Quebecoise (LSQ), Mexican Sign Language (MSL), Spanish Sign Language, and many, many others.

Not all deaf or hard-of-hearing people use sign language, spoken language, hearing aids, cochlear implants, or lip reading. Each person and family is unique and has their own preferences for how to communicate in different settings.

ABOUT THE AUTHOR

ANDREA BEATY is the bestselling author of the Questioneers series, as well as many other books, including *Dorko the Magnificent, Secrets of the Cicada Summer, Attack of the Fluffy Bunnies,* and *Happy Birthday, Madame Chapeau.* She has a degree in biology and computer science and spent many years in the computer industry. She now writes children's books in her home outside Chicago.

ABOUT THE ILLUSTRATOR

DAVID ROBERTS has illustrated many books, including the Questioneers series, *The Cook and the King,* and *Happy Birthday, Madame Chapeau.* He lives in London, where, when not drawing, he likes to make hats.

THREE CHEERS FOR

LILA GREER, TEACHER OF THE YEAR!

The new picture book from the bestselling series

THE QUESTIONEERS

COMING FALL 2023

COLLECT THEM ALL!